Bad, Bad
Bunnies

YOUNG YEARLING BOOKS YOU WILL ENJOY:

The Pee Wee Scout Books by Judy Delton

COOKIES AND CRUTCHES
CAMP GHOST-AWAY
LUCKY DOG DAYS
BLUE SKIES, FRENCH FRIES
GRUMPY PUMPKINS
PEANUT-BUTTER PILGRIMS
A PEE WEE CHRISTMAS
THAT MUSHY STUFF
SPRING SPROUTS
THE POOPED TROOP
THE PEE WEE JUBILEE
BAD, BAD BUNNIES

YEARLING BOOKS/YOUNG YEARLINGS/YEARLING CLASSICS are designed especially to entertain and enlighten young people. Patricia Reilly Giff, consultant to this series, received her bachelor's degree from Marymount College and a master's degree in history from St. John's University. She holds a Professional Diploma in Reading and a Doctorate of Humane Letters from Hofstra University. She was a teacher and reading consultant for many years, and is the author of numerous books for young readers.

For a complete listing of all Yearling titles,
write to Dell Readers Service,
P.O. Box 1045, South Holland, IL 60473.

Bad, Bad Bunnies

JUDY DELTON

Illustrated by Alan Tiegreen

A YOUNG YEARLING BOOK

Published by
Dell Publishing
a division of
Bantam Doubleday Dell Publishing Group, Inc.
1540 Broadway
New York, New York 10036

ISBN: 0-440-40278-6

Printed in the United States of America

March 1990

10 9 8

CWO

For Santi Udomkesmalee:
A reader, a winner
and a good Pee Wee Scout.

Contents

CHAPTER 1

The Fire Station

"Today," said Mrs. Peters, "we are going to the fire station. It is fire prevention week and we are going to learn how to prevent fires."

"My dad starts fires," said Roger White.

All of the Pee Wee Scouts stared at him.

"In our barbecue!" said Roger, laughing at his own joke.

The Pee Wees groaned. They were at their Tuesday Scout meeting at Mrs. Peters's house. The Scouts were seven years old. They were in second grade.

"It is all right to start a fire in your barbecue," said Mrs. Peters, who was their

Scout leader. "Because you are there to watch it."

"We start fires in our fireplace," said Rachel Meyers.

"That's all right too," Mrs. Peters said. "Today we are going to listen to the fire chief, and we are going to find out how to earn our fire safety badges."

Mrs. Peters's baby Nick jumped up and down in his jumper chair.

"Goo!" he said. He had a yellow marshmallow chicken in his hand. All of the Pee Wee Scouts had chickens to eat too.

"When are we going to dye Easter eggs, Mrs. Peters?" asked Molly Duff. "It's almost Easter."

"We will do that next week, Molly, when we talk about our Easter plans," Mrs. Peters answered. "Right now we have to think about fire prevention, and get ready to see the fire station."

The Scouts cheered. They liked to go on Scout outings.

"Do we get to ride on a fire engine?" asked Sonny Betz.

Sonny's mother shook her head. She was Mrs. Peters's helper. She came along to help when the Scouts went on trips.

"That sounds dangerous," Mrs. Betz said.

"She thinks everything is dangerous," whispered Mary Beth Kelly to Molly.

"Hey, you're not bringing that thing along to the fire station," said Roger, pointing to Sonny's pet hamster. Sonny carried it in his shirt pocket.

"Sure I am," said Sonny, stroking the hamster between its tiny ears.

Tracy Barnes sneezed. "I'm allergic to that thing!" she said.

"He's not a thing," said Sonny. "His name is Snuffy."

"He's full of germs," said Rachel. "I read that animals carry disease."

"I think he's cute," said Molly, petting the hamster. "Look at his cute little whiskers."

"Snuffy's going to be snuffed," said Roger, putting on his jacket. "He's going to be one dead weasel when he gets under the wheels of a fire truck."

Mrs. Peters looked at Roger and clapped her hands. "Let's remember our manners at the station, and be sure to thank the chief when we leave. Now we will all get in the van."

Mrs. Peters put Nick's jacket on him. Then she herded all the Scouts out of the door and into the van.

As they rode down the street to the station, Kevin Moe yelled, "Ring! Ring! Here we go to a fire!"

All the boys made siren noises all along the way.

At the fire station a man in a uniform came out to meet them. "I'm Larry Stone," he said. "The fire chief."

The Scouts scrambled into the station. The fire dog, Rusty, was asleep on the

5

seat of a big red fire truck. Mrs. Peters and Mrs. Betz helped the Scouts form a circle around Larry so they could hear what he had to say.

"First I want you to meet the other fire fighters," he said. "This is Dave."

Dave shook hands with all of the Scouts.

"And this is Carol," said Larry.

Carol had curly red hair. She smiled and shook hands too. Then Dave and Carol went back to work.

Larry said, "This is my rubber coat and hat." He put them on.

He put on his heavy rubber boots.

Then he told the Scouts exactly what happens when a fire alarm comes in to the station.

He told them what happens when the firemen get to the fire.

He showed them the hoses and the truck and let them all climb up on it.

"Do you rescue animals that get stuck up in trees?" ask Kenny Baker. "My aunt had a cat once that couldn't get down."

"Sometimes." Larry laughed.

Larry showed them the pole the firemen slid down to get to the truck.

"If a fire alarm comes in at night when the men are asleep upstairs, they get into their clothes and slide down to the truck in a matter of seconds," he said.

"Can we slide down?" asked Tim Noon.

Larry looked at Mrs. Peters and Mrs. Betz.

"If you are very careful," said Mrs. Peters.

Mrs. Betz looked doubtful.

"They won't get hurt," said Larry to Sonny's mother. "There's some foam padding at the bottom here."

"Hey, you're going to squish that rat in your pocket," Roger said to Sonny.

"Am not," said Sonny, patting his pocket.

The Scouts ran up the steps and lined up to slide down the pole. Kevin was first. Whiz! He zipped down the pole through the hole in the floor.

When Molly's turn came, she closed her eyes. She grasped the slippery pole tightly. Then she loosened her grip and in a minute she was on the ground!

"That was fun!" said Tracy, after her turn. "Can we do it again?"

Larry laughed. "I have something else in mind," he said, winking at Mrs. Betz.

Lisa Ronning walked over to Molly.

"Look at Sonny's shirt pocket," she whispered.

Molly looked. So did Mary Beth.

"There's nothing in it," whispered Molly. "Oh, no."

"He's probably holding Snuffy in his hand," said Mary Beth.

Sonny grabbed the pole and swung around it.

"No, he isn't," said Lisa.

Larry was talking and talking. He was telling the Scouts about preventing fires.

"I haven't seen Snuffy since Sonny slid down the pole," said Lisa.

Rat's knees, thought Molly. Where is that little hamster with the whiskers?

CHAPTER 2

Hamster Alert!

"We better tell him," said Lisa.

"Not me," said Mary Beth.

"Maybe we should tell Mrs. Peters," said Molly.

The girls looked at Mrs. Peters. She was listening closely to what Larry was saying. Mrs. Betz was listening to Larry too.

"Sonny will find out in a minute," said Mary Beth. "By himself."

Mary Beth was right.

"HELP!" screamed Sonny, pulling at his pocket. "HELP! Snuffy is gone! He's lost!"

"What did I tell you?" said Roger.

Sonny began to cry. Softly at first. Then louder and louder.

"What a baby," said Tracy.

"It's awful to lose a pet," said Molly.

Larry raised his arm. "Keep calm, everyone. We will find him if he is in the station."

"The door is wide open," said Kenny.

Sonny put his head in his mother's lap. He was wailing.

"Let's all look around carefully," said Mrs. Peters, lifting a pile of hoses.

The Scouts looked under the fire engine.

They looked in the firemen's rubber boots.

They looked behind desks and under ladders.

Molly even looked outside in the bushes.

"He's a goner," said Roger.

"You can get another one at the pet store," said Kevin.

12

Sonny cried louder. "I don't want another one, I want Snuffy!"

He sat on a chair and sobbed. Larry brought cans of cold soda pop for Sonny and Mrs. Betz.

Suddenly Rusty, the fire dog, barked.

"Arf, arf!" His hair seemed to stand up on his back.

He jumped off the fire truck and dashed through the door.

"He's chasing Snuffy!" shouted Sonny. "I saw him!"

All of the Scouts raced out of the door after Rusty. The little hamster was running for his life, with the dog right behind him.

"He's scared!" yelled Sonny. "Snuffy's scared!"

Just as Rusty caught up to Snuffy, the hamster dashed up a large oak tree. Rusty stood with his front paws on the trunk and barked and barked. "Arf! Arf!"

Snuffy sat on one of the branches and trembled.

"Poor thing," said Molly.

"He is cute," said Patty Baker, Kenny's twin sister.

The Scouts all gathered around the oak tree and waited.

"He can't get down," said Sonny, still crying.

"We don't have to worry," said Kenny. "That's what the fire department is for. To rescue pets from trees. Snuffy knew what he was doing when he went up a tree in the firemen's yard."

Larry laughed. "I guess we can get him down."

The Scouts watched while he and another fireman brought out a long ladder. And a slice of bread. They set the ladder up beside the tree. Larry began to climb. Higher and higher and higher.

15

But the higher Larry climbed, the higher Snuffy went!

"He's way up in the sky!" said Tim.

"Here, Snuffy!" called Sonny. "Come on, Snuffy."

Larry held some bread up to the hamster but Snuffy didn't budge. So Larry climbed up even higher. He was almost at the top of the tree now.

"He doesn't like bread," called Sonny. "He wants nuts."

"He'll never make it," said Roger.

Suddenly Larry reached out his hand and grabbed Snuffy. He popped him into his pocket and climbed down the ladder.

The Scouts cheered. "Hooray! You saved him."

"How can we thank you?" said Mrs. Peters.

Larry handed the pet over to Sonny. "All in a day's work," he said.

Sonny smiled.

"Now for my surprise!" said Larry. "Who would like a ride in the engine?"

"Me!" shouted every Scout, racing to climb on.

"I'll wait here and hold Snuffy," said Mrs. Betz.

Mrs. Peters sat in the front seat next to Larry. She held Nick on her lap.

Off they went.

Down one street and up another.

Rusty stood on the backseat with his head sticking out of the window. His long ears blew in the wind.

"Put the siren on!" shouted Kevin.

Larry turned on the siren, but only for a little while. "It's illegal to use it unless there is a fire," he said.

Larry drove the red fire engine past their school, and past Tim's house. Past the theater and back to the station.

Then the Scouts thanked Larry and they all said good-bye.

17

As the Scouts climbed into the van, Molly noticed that Larry was talking to Mrs. Betz more than anyone else.

"I think Larry likes Sonny's mother," she whispered to Tracy. "His parents are divorced."

"Really?" said Tracy.

Everyone waited while Mrs. Betz stood outside talking to Larry.

"Come on, Mom!" yelled Sonny.

Finally Mrs. Betz got into the van. "Sorry," she said, with a big smile.

When the Scouts got to Mrs. Peters's house, they sat down in her living room. Mrs. Peters said, "Next week is spring vacation, but we will meet on Tuesday as usual. I want you each to bring three hard-boiled eggs with you to our meeting."

The Scouts listened quietly to Mrs. Peters.

"Vacation is a good time to start to earn your fire safety badge," she explained. "First of all, you must draw a picture of something you saw at the station today. Next, you must check to see if you have a smoke alarm in your home. And then you must watch for any fire hazards. And if you ever see a fire, or a dangerous situation, be sure to report it to your parents or to the fire station."

Molly knew there was a smoke alarm in her house. And she could draw a picture of a fire truck. That was easy.

But where was she going to find a fire hazard?

CHAPTER 3
Hunting for a Hazard

On the way home Tracy said, "Maybe we can work on our badge together. You and Mary Beth and me."

"Okay," said Molly. "I'll meet you in the park tomorrow."

The next morning the girls sat on a bench together. The sun was shining and the day was already warm. They wondered where to start.

"We don't have a smoke detector," said Tracy.

"We do," said Molly. "You better tell

your mom to get one. I drew my picture of the fire truck."

"Mine is of Snuffy," said Mary Beth. "He was the best part of the trip."

"Where can we look for fire hazards?" asked Molly. "I've got the number of the fire department right here." She patted her back pocket. "When we see one we can call Larry right away. Then we'll have proof, for our badge."

"Let's close our eyes and think of where most fires are," said Tracy.

The girls thought and thought.

"Maybe we will just have to go looking," said Mary Beth. "We can't find a fire here in the park."

The girls walked up one street and down another. They looked in backyards and front yards. They looked in the windows of stores, and in gas stations.

"Look!" said Tracy. "Is that a hazard?"

She pointed to a man in the middle of

the street. He was digging a hole with a loud machine. The machine was shooting sparks out into the air.

"Those sparks look dangerous," admitted Mary Beth. "I think we should warn him."

Tracy marched up to the man. He put his arm out and said, "Stay away! This is dangerous!"

"I know it is!" shouted Tracy. "That's why I'm here."

"What's that?" shouted the man. "I can't hear you."

"Those sparks are a fire hazard. You have to stop digging that hole this minute! Or I'm going to report you."

The man put his hand behind his ear and shook his head. "Stay away," he kept saying.

"I am going to report him," said Tracy. She called Larry from a pay phone.

He told her he would check out the situation.

"You were lucky," said Molly. "Those sparks are a real hazard."

The girls walked and walked. They stopped at Tracy's house for a snack. Then they walked up and down some more streets.

One old house had lots of junk in the yard.

"Mrs. Peters said junk is a hazard," said Mary Beth.

"Not a real good one, though," said Molly. "There isn't actually any fire or sparks."

The girls agreed. "I want one as good as yours," said Mary Beth to Tracy. "One with real fire."

"Let's stop and get a candy bar at the store," said Molly.

When the girls went through the parking lot to the grocery store, Mary Beth cried, "Look!"

The girls stopped. There was a fire right in front of them. A huge fire! Orange flames were shooting into the air!

"Rat's knees!" cried Molly.

"He's burning boxes," said Tracy. "In that big oven."

"It's an incinerator," said Mary Beth. "And the door is wide open. Anybody could get burned. All these cars could get burned! We better warn him."

Tracy ran up to the man with the boxes.

She pulled on his apron.

"Stand back!" he shouted. "This is dangerous!"

Tracy ran back. "He knows it's dangerous," she said.

"Then why doesn't he put it out?" asked Molly.

Mary Beth went up to him this time. "That is a fire hazard," she said.

24

The fire was crackling and popping and spitting.

"Stay out of the way, kids," said the man.

"We are reporting you!" said Mary Beth, turning around to leave.

At the next pay phone Mary Beth called Larry and told him about the hazard.

"I still don't have a one," said Molly.

"We'll find another one," said Tracy. "Don't worry."

The girls walked and walked.

They looked and looked.

There was no sign of a fire hazard anywhere.

"It's getting late," said Tracy. "I have to go home."

Molly felt terrible.

"We'll find you one tomorrow," Mary Beth said. "We have lots of time during vacation."

"It sounded like Larry was laughing

when I called," said Mary Beth. "Why would he laugh at a fire hazard?"

"Well, we did the right thing," said Tracy. "And we can get our fire safety badge on Tuesday."

CHAPTER 4

Bad Bunny Sonny

But Mrs. Peters did not give badges on Tuesday. She had Easter on her mind.

"We will wait until everyone is ready," she said, "and give the badges out all together. Today the good word is *Easter*."

Good, thought Molly. More time to find a hazard.

The Scouts gave their eggs to Mrs. Peters.

Then they talked about fire safety.

Then they told all of the good deeds they had done for others during the week.

"Now," said Mrs. Peters, "we are going to dye Easter eggs. We'll put some of them in baskets for poor children, and hang some on our Easter egg tree. The others we will save for our Easter egg hunt on Saturday."

"Miss Peters," Tracy called, "will there be a prize for the one who finds the most eggs at the hunt?"

"Yes, Tracy. The one who finds the most eggs will get a big stuffed Easter bunny, and the one who comes in second will get a box of chocolate cream eggs."

"My dad says chocolate is bad for your teeth," said Rachel.

Rachel's father was a dentist.

"No way," said Kevin. "I eat chocolate and I have good teeth."

He pulled his lips back with his fingers to show Rachel his teeth.

Mrs. Peters clapped her hands for attention.

The Pee Wees went down in the Peters's basement. On a big table were little jars with Easter egg dyes in them. There were ten place mats. And on each place mat were dyes for every Scout.

Red. Blue. Green. Yellow. Orange. Pink. Purple.

There were wax crayons to write on the eggs.

There were little stickers with swirly designs to decorate the eggs.

And there were pictures to paste on the eggs.

"I have some extra hard-boiled eggs here," said Mrs. Peters. "So with the three you each brought, we have plenty for the egg hunt and the baskets."

Mrs. Peters showed them how to dip the eggs in the dye. She told them how long to leave them in.

"Where is Sonny?" whispered Tracy to Molly.

Sonny's spot at the table was empty.

"Maybe he is sick," said Molly.

Just as the Scouts were deciding on their favorite color, there was the sound of voices upstairs.

The Scouts could hear Sonny's voice. But who was with him?

Sonny came down the steps. He had Snuffy in his pocket and his three eggs in a bag. But he looked angry.

Mrs. Betz came in behind him.

And behind her was Larry, the fire chief.

"What is he doing here?" yelled Kenny.

Mrs. Peters looked surprised too.

"Larry drove us over," said Mrs. Betz. "We went out on a call with him."

"It was a false alarm!" Larry laughed.

Sonny scowled.

Larry and Mrs. Betz waved good-bye as they left.

"I am going to dye every egg red," said Patty. "It's my favorite color."

31

Molly liked red too. But it didn't seem like an Easter color to her. "I am going to make one pink, and one blue, and one yellow," she said.

The Scouts worked hard.

Suddenly Tim cried, "Hey! Sonny bumped my arm and cracked my egg."

"Did not, liar!" said Sonny.

Mrs. Peters gave Tim a new egg. "Maybe Sonny needs more room," she said, frowning at him.

Everyone moved over to give Sonny more room.

Rachel drew a face on her egg. "This is me," she said.

"Egghead Rachel!" teased Roger. "Rachel is an egghead."

Rachel pretended she was going to throw an egg at Roger.

But she didn't.

"My purple egg is missing!" said Mary

Beth. She looked around the table. There it was, in front of Sonny.

"Sonny took it," she said.

"I did not," said Sonny.

"I know that's mine," said Mary Beth to Molly. "I pasted Donald Duck on it. And it's purple. It's my favorite egg."

Mrs. Peters gave Mary Beth a new egg. She frowned at Sonny again.

"What's the matter with Sonny?" Molly asked Lisa. "He's sure a grumpy pumpkin today."

Lisa just shrugged her shoulders.

When Molly finished dyeing her third egg, she reached for some extras.

Snuffy was sitting on the worktable. He began to walk around the eggs.

"Look!" said Lisa.

Snuffy had stopped in front of Roger. Quick as a wink Roger grabbed Snuffy and dipped his backside in purple dye.

Molly and Lisa watched.

Sonny didn't see him, though. He was cutting out a picture of a rabbit.

Roger swished Snuffy's bottom around and around. When he took it out, his stubby tail was bright purple.

"Ho, ho, Snuffy's an Easter bunny now!" shouted Roger.

"Oh, no!" shouted Sonny. He turned red with anger. "I'll get you for that!" Sonny picked up an Easter egg and threw it at Roger.

The egg missed Roger.

But it hit Mrs. Peters!

Splat! The egg broke and ran down Mrs. Peters's blouse.

No one said a word.

Everyone stared.

Mrs. Peters marched over to Sonny and gave him a little shake.

"Why are you such a bad bunny today?" she asked. "It's almost Easter. What's bothering you?"

Sonny put his head down and began to cry.

Molly got some paper towels and helped Mrs. Peters sponge off her blouse.

"Yuck," said Rachel. "Sonny, didn't you know we were supposed to bring cooked eggs?"

"Why aren't your eggs cooked, Sonny?" asked Mrs. Peters.

"My mom forgot," sobbed Sonny.

Mrs. Peters went upstairs and when she came down she had a clean blouse on. She had baby Nick with her. She patted Sonny on the head. "It was just an accident," she said.

"He threw it on purpose," said Tracy. "He's mean."

"Yeah," said Roger. "He's a bad, bad bunny."

The Scouts finished dyeing their eggs. Mrs. Peters hung some of them on the egg tree with little ribbons. She put the others in baskets with marshmallow rabbits and jelly beans. The Scouts got to take their favorite egg home with them.

Soon it was time to hold hands and sing the Pee Wee Scout song. And say the Pee Wee Scout pledge. Then everyone helped clean up the basement.

"Saturday is the Easter-egg hunt," Mrs. Peters reminded them. "Be at the park at ten o'clock in the morning."

Outside, Mrs. Betz and Larry were waiting in the car for Sonny.

"This is mysterious," said Mary Beth. "Why is the fire chief hanging around here?"

"Maybe he thinks the Pee Wee Scouts are going to catch on fire," Kevin said, laughing.

"You guys are really dumb," said Rachel. "He's dating Mrs. Betz."

CHAPTER 5

The Winner

All week Molly looked for a fire hazard.

All week she didn't find one.

On Saturday morning the sun was shining.

"It's a wonderful day for an Easter-egg hunt," said Mrs. Duff.

Molly's mother gave her a basket to take with her, for the eggs she would find. Maybe Molly would find the most eggs! She raced to the park.

"Happy Easter!" called Mrs. Peters, as the Scouts gathered.

"Look at the balloons!" shouted Lisa.

"Mrs. Betz and Larry decorated the

park," said Mrs. Peters. "And they hid the eggs."

Mrs. Betz and Larry.

Molly started to understand why Sonny was upset.

When all of the Scouts were there, Mrs. Peters said, "Now, don't dig, or step on any plants while you are looking for eggs. They are all where you can find them easily. I don't want to see any bad bunnies today." She smiled.

Molly could see one red egg already. It was under a pine tree.

"Ready, set, go!" shouted Mrs. Peters.

The Scouts scattered.

Molly headed for the pine tree. She grabbed the red egg. Then she looked under rosebushes and in back of the toolshed. She found another one under a park bench. A yellow one.

Around and around the Scouts ran.

In every direction.

Soon Molly had five eggs in her basket.

"I can't find any," Tim whined.

Molly felt like giving Tim one of hers, but that wouldn't be fair. "Look in back of that birdhouse," she whispered to him.

"I found six," said Rachel. "I hope I win that rabbit."

"I have six too," said Kenny.

"I have to find one more," said Rachel.

Molly looked around for Sonny. Finally she saw him sitting on a stump. He wasn't even looking for eggs.

Molly sat down beside him.

"Get out of here," he said.

"What's the matter, Sonny?"

"None of your beeswax," he answered.

"It's Larry, isn't it?" said Molly.

"I hate him!" said Sonny. "He's always hanging around our house and my mom goes out with him and leaves me with a baby-sitter."

Sonny punched his fist into his hand.

"She used to take me with her. Now she forgets to make my breakfast and everything."

Molly wondered what to say.

"I wish that old fire chief would get out of town," Sonny went on. Then he got up and ran off.

"What's the matter with him, anyway?" Roger asked Molly.

Molly didn't answer. She didn't want anyone to tease Sonny about his mother's boyfriend.

"I found another egg!" said Rachel, walking by. "I bet I'll be the winner with seven."

Mrs. Peters sat on the bench in the sun. Beside her sat the large white stuffed rabbit. The first prize.

"Ten more minutes!" she called.

The Scouts scampered around to be sure all the eggs had been found.

Sonny had no eggs.

Molly watched him pout.

Then Mrs. Peters called, "Time is up! Time to count the eggs and find out who is the winner!"

The Pee Wees brought their baskets over to Mrs. Peters. They all talked at once.

"I think I'm the winner, Mrs. Peters," said Rachel.

"Rachel has seven eggs," said Mrs. Peters. "Does anyone have more than seven?"

Rachel looked nervous.

Patty raised her hand. Patty was shy. Her voice was so soft, the Scouts could hardly hear her. "I have ten," she said.

"Does anyone have more than ten?" called Mrs. Peters.

No one did.

"Our winner," said Mrs. Peters, "is Patty Baker, with ten eggs!"

She held up Patty's basket and the Scouts cheered.

"Yeah, Patty!" called Roger.

Mrs. Peters handed the prize to Patty.

"Thank you," she said softly. She gave the rabbit a hug.

"And in second place," said Mrs. Peters, "we have Kevin Moe! With a total of eight eggs!"

"Thank you, thank you," said Kevin, as if he had won an election.

"He doesn't have to give a speech just because he won a box of candy," scoffed Tracy.

Mrs. Peters passed out the balloons and decorations. "And you can take the eggs you found home with you," she said.

"Thanks a lot," Rachel muttered.

The Pee Wees joined hands and sang their Pee Wee Scout song and said their Pee Wee Scout pledge.

Then it was time to go home.

Molly walked with Tracy and Mary Beth. Sonny was walking alone. He was kicking a rock ahead of him.

"I think we should try to cheer Sonny up," said Molly.

"Why?" said Tracy. "He's a baby. And he's been mean lately."

"He's unhappy," said Molly. She told her friends about Larry.

"He's jealous," said Mary Beth. "I sometimes get jealous of my brother."

"There must be something we can do to help," said Molly. "Our song says Scouts are helpers."

"Maybe somebody can get Larry transferred to another town," said Tracy. "My uncle got transferred once."

"We don't want to get *rid* of Larry. We want Sonny and Larry to be friends," said Molly.

"Molly's right," said Mary Beth. "Sonny

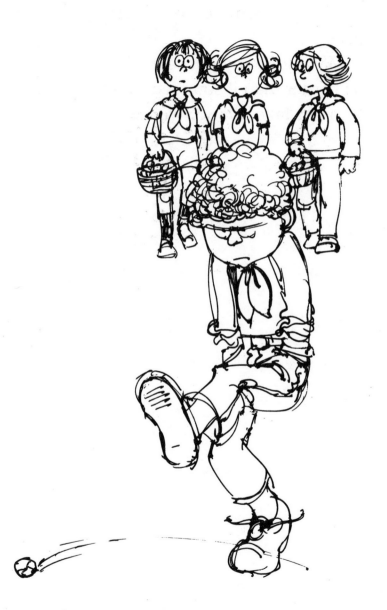

is kind of a baby. Larry could be good for him."

Making Sonny and Larry friends could be harder than it sounded, thought Molly. It might take a lot of work.

CHAPTER 6

Molly Smells Trouble

On Easter Sunday Molly's grandparents came to dinner. They brought Molly baskets full of candy. And two stuffed animals. After dinner she called Tracy.

"I have to help with the dishes," said Tracy when Molly asked her to go for a bike ride. "But I'll meet you at three o'clock."

Later that day the girls rode their bikes to the park. Kevin was there playing ball with Roger. And Mary Beth was playing a game with her family.

Pretty soon Sonny came along. He had Snuffy in his pocket. Snuffy still had a purple body. Sonny rode his bike. The one with training wheels on it.

"Hi," called Molly.

Sonny didn't answer.

"Let's go cheer him up," said Molly. "It will count as a good deed."

"It must be nice to have a fire chief in the family," said Molly politely.

"He's not in the family," said Sonny. "He's a stranger."

"She means it would be fun to have a fire chief for a friend," said Tracy. "In case there's a fire in your house or something."

Sonny pouted.

"Lots of families have more than just two people in them," Molly went on. "I mean, I've got a dad and you don't see me getting mad about it."

"So do I," said Tracy. "It's not so bad."

"Larry's not my dad!" shouted Sonny.

"Well, he might be someday," said Molly.

Sonny didn't answer.

"I think you should get used to him," said Tracy. "He could do stuff with you. He's a nice guy."

Sonny glared at her.

"Let's go," said Tracy.

Before they left, Molly whispered, "Your mom still loves you, Sonny. She just needs a grown-up friend too."

"I have to go," said Tracy. "I'm playing Monopoly with my aunt."

Tracy waved and rode off.

Molly watched Roger and Kevin. She played with Mary Beth's family awhile. Then she decided to go on a bike ride herself.

She rode up one street.

Down another.

Past the drugstore.

Around the church.

It was a wonderful sunny day.

A perfect day for a bike ride.

I'll ride down alleys, Molly said to herself. I'll look at the backs of houses instead of the fronts.

Up and down.

Up and down.

Molly had not seen these backyards before. It was fun to see new things. No one was out in the yards. They are all in the house eating Easter dinner, thought Molly. Or watching Easter specials on TV. Or taking naps. That's what her grandma was doing.

As Molly rode, she sniffed the air. She smelled something besides lilacs. It reminded her of the Pee Wee weenie roast last year. The smell got stronger as Molly rode on.

Then she saw smoke.

The smoke was curling out from under a garage door. No one was around. Molly's first thought was to call the fire chief. Would Larry be at the firehouse on Easter?

More and more smoke filled the alley. There was no time to go home and tell her parents.

Molly parked her bike and ran to the back door of the house. She pounded on the door.

"Help!" she shouted.

An old man came to the door.

"Your garage is on fire!" she shouted.

"Come in!" he said to Molly.

He picked up the telephone and called 911. He told them about the fire and gave his address.

Before long Molly heard sirens, and the fire truck came around the corner. It looked like the fire truck that the Scouts had ridden in not long ago.

Molly and the man stayed in the house as the fire fighters dragged their hoses to

the garage. Dave and Carol were there. Larry too.

After a while Larry came into the house.

"Molly Duff!" said Larry. "Do you live here?"

Molly told him how she was riding by and saw the smoke.

"If you hadn't reported that when you did," said Larry, "it would have spread to the car and exploded. But you caught it early. It was a pile of old rags burning in the corner of the garage."

"I must have dropped an ash from my pipe when I put my car away," said the man, whose name was Mr. Harmon. "You saved my car, Molly. And my garage."

"And you kept the fire from spreading to nearby houses," said Larry. "You are a hero. I think the evening news would like to hear about this!"

Molly couldn't believe it.

As Larry drove her home in the fire

engine, she remembered something else. A pile of old rags was a fire hazard. She would get her badge!

"You found a fire hazard, all right," Carol said.

"And I wasn't even looking for it," said Molly.

CHAPTER 7

The TV Pee Wee

Molly told her parents and grand-parents about the fire.

Then she called her friends. "I'll be able to get my fire safety badge!" she told Tracy. She called Mary Beth and said the same thing over again.

As soon as she hung up, the phone rang. It was Channel Five News. "We would like to have your daughter on our news show," said the reporter to Mr. Duff. "Could she be here at five o'clock?"

"We'll be there," said Molly's dad.

Molly was speechless.

"What will you wear?" asked her mother.

"My blouse and Pee Wee Scout kerchief," said Molly.

Molly's grandma helped her get ready.

At a quarter of five Larry drove up to take them to the station.

"What an Easter surprise this is!" said Molly's grandpa, getting into the fire chief's car. "We never thought Molly would be on television today."

When they got to the station, Larry called Mrs. Peters. Mrs. Peters called all the Scouts. She told them to watch the news on Channel Five.

Molly's family sat on folding chairs in the studio. Molly and Larry sat on the stage. Bright lights shone in their faces. When the news started, the newsman said, "Tonight we have an Easter heroine right here in our own town. Molly Duff, age seven, was responsible for averting a catastrophe this afternoon. She stopped a

fire that could have spread throughout an entire neighborhood.

"We will be back to talk with Molly herself, after this commercial."

Then a commercial with dancing cats came on the TV monitor. "Scampies cat food will make your cat dance too!" the man said.

Then all of a sudden the screen switched to Mr. Harmon, standing by the pile of rags in his garage.

"If Molly Duff hadn't come to tell me about the smoke, my new car would have gone up in flames," he said. "She's some Scout, all right!"

"And now we switch live to our studio, where we have Molly Duff and the fire chief, Larry Stone."

The newsman put a microphone in front of Larry. Larry said almost the same thing as Mr. Harmon.

"And how do you feel about being a

local heroine?" said the newsman to Molly.

Molly stood up straight. Her Pee Wee kerchief looked neat around her neck. "Scouts are helpers," she said. "I was glad to do a good deed, and I'm glad I can get my fire safety badge now too."

"And here to present that badge to Molly is our fire chief again, Larry Stone."

Larry pinned the badge on Molly's blouse. "Congratulations!" he said. "We are proud of you."

Molly was the first one of the Scouts to get her badge. And the only one to get it on TV!

After the news broadcast Molly's family applauded. Her mother and dad hugged her.

The news reporter got some coffee for Larry and the Duffs. Then he showed Molly's family around the studio.

Something was bothering Molly. Something she had to tell Larry. She wanted to help Sonny. She tried to think of what to say. And how to say it.

"Sonny is jealous," she blurted out. "His mother used to do things with him. Now she does things with you."

Larry looked surprised. He thought for a minute. "It's very good of you to tell me, Molly," he said. "I'm sorry I didn't think of that."

"Please don't tell Sonny I told you," said Molly. "Or Mrs. Betz."

"It will be our secret," he said.

Molly wanted to tell Larry that Sonny would like him, if he got to know him, but there was no time. Her family was through with the tour. It was time to go.

Everyone piled into Larry's fire car, and they drove home.

The three adults chattered away while Molly worried. Maybe she should have minded her own business about Sonny.

Soon they drove up to the Duff's house.
As Molly got out, Larry said, "Thank you,
Molly."

And he winked at her.

Was that a good sign?

CHAPTER 8

A Secret Good Deed

When the Duffs got into the house, the phone began to ring.

It rang and rang and rang.

Mrs. Peters called.

Mary Beth called.

Molly's teacher called.

Mrs. Betz called.

Everyone had seen Molly on TV!

Finally Mrs. Duff said, "I think it is time for bed. This has been a very busy Easter Sunday."

Molly tossed and turned after she went to bed. When she finally fell asleep, she dreamed she was on TV and Sonny kept throwing eggs at her.

"Stop!" she was calling out when she awoke in the morning.

Would Sonny find out she had told Larry? Would he throw eggs at her at the meeting on Tuesday?

It would not be long until she found out.

When Tuesday came she went into Mrs. Peters's house for the meeting. All of the Scouts began to clap. There was a sign on the wall, saying CONGRATULATIONS, MOLLY.

"Did they put makeup on you?" asked Roger.

"Were you scared?" asked Tim.

"My cousin was on TV," said Lisa.

Molly told them all about it. When she was through, they ate cupcakes. And leftover marshmallow Easter eggs.

"And now," said Mrs. Peters, "we will hand out the rest of the fire safety badges."

She called all of the Scouts' names, and they all went up for their badges.

Molly didn't see Sonny. Where could he be? Maybe he and Mrs. Betz had moved away because they were so unhappy. Maybe Molly had caused some trouble.

"I think my fire hazard was just as dangerous as yours," said Tracy. "That machine was real fire, not just smoke. And I didn't get to be on TV."

"It's not as dangerous," said Mary Beth. "Because the man was there. No one knew about Molly's fire."

Molly squeezed Mary Beth's hand. Mary Beth was still her best friend. She always knew what to say to make Molly feel good.

"Now we will tell some good deeds," said Mrs. Peters.

"I got gum out of my brother's hair!" shouted Tim.

"Yuck," said Rachel. "That sounds icky."

"I gave an Easter egg to the lady next door," said Lisa.

"Good for you both," said Mrs. Peters.

"Mrs. Peters," called Rachel, "Molly has the best good deed of all. She saved a garage from burning down."

Molly felt shy. Her fire hazard was a good deed. But she didn't want to report it.

"Rachel is right. Stopping a fire is a wonderful good deed."

"It's better than pulling gum out of somebody's hair," scoffed Roger with a sneer.

"All good deeds are important," said Mrs. Peters.

Just then Sonny burst in the door.

He did not throw eggs.

He did not trip anyone.

He was smiling.

"I'm sorry I'm late," he said. "I was at a ball game with Larry. The Twins won, but the game was tied. We had to stay for extra innings."

Sonny had a Twins hat on, and a pennant in the pocket of his shirt. In his other pocket was Snuffy. And he wasn't purple anymore.

All the Pee Wee Scouts held hands and sang the Pee Wee Scout song. Then they said the Pee Wee Scout pledge.

"I think it worked," whispered Tracy to Molly. "We did help Sonny. Look how happy he is today!"

Molly nodded. She wouldn't tell anyone the secret.

It was one good deed she would never report.

Pee Wee Scout Song

(to the tune of
"Old MacDonald Had a Farm")

Scouts are helpers, Scouts have fun
Pee Wee, Pee Wee Scouts!
We sing and play when work is done,
Pee Wee, Pee Wee Scouts!

With a good deed here,
And an errand there,
Here a hand, there a hand,
Everywhere a good hand.

Scouts are helpers, Scouts have fun,
Pee Wee, Pee Wee Scouts!

 Pee Wee Scout Pledge

We love our country
And our home,
Our school and neighbors too.

As Pee Wee Scouts
We pledge our best
In everything we do.